CREOLE
written by: Stephen Cosgrove
illustrated by: Robin James

A Serendipity Book

Published by Creative Education, Inc., 123 South Broad Street, Mankato, Minnesota 56001. Copyright ©1975 by Serendipity Communications, Ltd. Printed in the United States of America. All rights reserved.

Library of Congress Cataloging in Publication Data

Cosgrove, Stephen.
  Creole.

  SUMMARY: Because Creole is ugly, the other animals assume she is mean until they realize their mistake.
    [1. Beauty, Personal—Fiction.   2. Friendship—Fiction]
I. James, Robin.   II. Title.
PZ7.C8187Cr 1978   [E]   78-11182
ISBN 0-87191-655-X

Dedicated to Farrell Brown, a man of many names and many faces.

On a foggy, foggy morning in the land of the swamp, from a battered, speckled egg, Creole was born.

She was big, fat and very, very ugly. She had warts on her fingers, warts on her toes, boney pointed knees and a big flat nose.

Beneath all of that which made her so ugly was the most beautiful heart that had ever beat anywhere in the world.

Because of her beautiful heart, Creole thought the most beautiful thoughts that could ever be thought. She thought of love, for her heart was full of love. She thought of happiness, for her heart was full of happiness. And she thought of tenderness, for she was the gentlest of all the creatures.

Day in and day out she would sit alone sniffing the flowers and talking to the trees that grew in the swamp.

One day as she was sitting near a large magnolia tree, Creole thought, "Maybe I should share my love and happiness with the other creatures of the swamp."

So, with that in mind she set off to find some animals that could become her friends.

As noisy as that swamp could be with all the animals living there, it would fall into a silent hush as Creole walked by. The birds became quiet, the possum sat still, and the alligators all slipped away. They all thought that because she was so fat and ugly, she just had to be mean too!

Creole looked and looked but she could not find a friend at all. Finally, with watermelon-size tears falling at her feet, she sat with a heavy thump on a big old broken stump and cried and cried.

"Why won't anyone listen to me?" she sobbed. "The only thing I want in the whole world is just to have someone to tell my happy thoughts to!"

The tears rolled over her cheeks, bounced off her belly, slipped and slid down the log, and finally landed with a large ker-plunk on the head of a baby alligator sitting just below.

The little alligator looked around to see who had been throwing water on him when suddenly, from above, came another large tear, ker-plunk! He looked up, way up, and saw Creole.

"Why are you cr-crying on me?" stuttered the alligator.

Creole looked down and spied the smallest, most pathetic alligator she had ever seen. "I'm sorry," she sobbed. "I didn't know you were down there. The last thing I wanted to do in the whole world was to hurt someone."

Wiping a tear from her eye, Creole suddenly realized that the little alligator had not run away and was actually talking with her. "Why didn't you run away like everyone else?" asked Creole.

"Because I h-h-hope you will be my f-friend," stuttered the alligator. "The other alligators all l-laugh at me because I stutter and can't talk straight."

They looked into each other's eyes and realized that they were what each of them was looking for...a friend.

For the longest time, Creole and her new-found friend sat and shared their friendship.

After a while Creole said, "It's too bad you and I don't have more friends. I wonder what we could do to convince the other creatures not to laugh at you and not to be afraid of me?"

The little alligator nodded his head in agreement, and the two of them tried to figure out a way to talk with the other animals of the swamp.

"I know what we shall do," Creole said. "I can hide behind a big bush and you can stand in front. When all the animals have gathered around, I'll tell you what to say. Then you can talk about love and happiness."

Well, the little alligator reluctantly agreed and with Creole hidden behind a lilac bush, he nervously called to the other animals. A couple of times he got so scared he tried to hide, but each time she would gently shove him back out and tell him not to be afraid.

Now the other animals of the swamp, not seeing Creole around, knew that it was safe to come out and listen to all that the little alligator had to say. One by one they all crept from the bushes, the berries and the waters of the swamp.

There were four or five big old alligators and a couple of small ones, two yellow snakes and a blue one, twenty-three birds of a feather, a lazy possum and his wife, and a great white heron.

With all the creatures gathered around, the little alligator began repeating what Creole was whispering to him. He told them about the beauty of the early morning dawn and about the sunset over the swamp. He talked of love, béauty and most of all, friendship.

The animals were all amazed at what the alligator was saying and how clearly he was saying it. For you see, when the alligator didn't have to make up what he said, he didn't stutter at all.

Everything would have been all right if it had not been for a nosey squirrel who happened to peek behind the bush that Creole was whispering from. The squirrel let out a yelp and shouted, "Run as fast as you can! The big, ugly creature is back!"

Creole was so shocked at being discovered that she tripped on the bush, scaring the creatures even more. "Wait! Wait!" she cried. "I'm not going to hurt you. We just wanted to be your friends!"

But the creatures wouldn't listen and scrambling over one another, they ran away.

The little alligator chased after them, shouting in a very clear voice, "Stop! Creole is my friend and she would never hurt anyone!"

The other creatures, who by this time were hidden in the bushes, listened to the little alligator and suddenly a wise old owl spoke from the branches over a pine tree: "Perhaps we should believe him," he said, "for his ugly friend, Creole, has stopped him from stuttering."

Sure enough, during all the excitement of chasing the creatures, the little alligator hadn't stuttered a single word.

Sheepishly all the creatures went back to where Creole was sadly waiting, with the little alligator leading the way. "Creole," said the alligator, "all my fellow creatures of the swamp are sorry that they judged you by how you look, but if you will forgive them, they would love to hear you talk of all the happiness in your heart."

With a radiant smile overcoming her tears, Creole hugged each and every one of the creatures and made them all her friends.

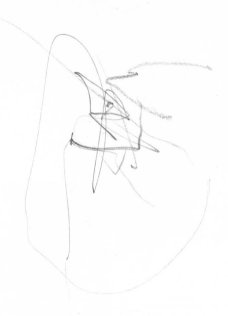

Never judge someone
By the way he looks
Or a book by the way it's covered;
For inside those tattered pages,
There's a lot to be discovered.